This Walker book belongs to:

For three special women
Beryl Ferrier, Lennie's little sister, who shared her childhood with me,
Julie Oliveri, who first told me the story and Maryann Ballantyne,
who believed in this book from the start.
CF

To the memory of my brother, friend and mentor,
John McLean
20 June 1929 — 03 March 2019
AM

First published in 2020
by Black Dog Books
an imprint of Walker Books Australia Pty Ltd
Locked Bag 22, Newtown
NSW 2042 Australia
www.walkerbooks.com.au

This edition published in 2021.

A catalogue record for this book is available from the National Library of Australia

ISBN: 978 1 760654 44 3

The illustrations for this book were created with pencil and watercolour.
Photos of Lennie and Ginger Mick from the collection of
The Leongatha Historical Society and reproduced with their kind permission.
Typeset in Mrs Eaves

Printed and bound in China

3 5 7 9 8 6 4

To the Bridge

The Journey of Lennie and Ginger Mick

On Lennie's second birthday his grandfather gave him a pony. Ginger Mick had been born on the very same day as Lennie.

By Corinne Fenton *Illustrated by* Andrew McLean

WALKER BOOKS
AND SUBSIDIARIES
LONDON • BOSTON • SYDNEY • AUCKLAND

Each day bundles of newspapers were tossed from the steam train as it passed Gwyther's Siding. Lennie was always there with Ginger Mick, first to read the news of Australia's biggest bridge.

He wanted to know everything about it – how the giant arches were designed, how they clung to the pylons and how the bridge would carry trucks, trains – all kinds of transport. And how it would stand strong into the future.

One winter's afternoon Lennie's dad fell while ploughing the paddocks. He broke his leg badly, which meant he would be away for months in a Melbourne hospital.

Early each morning Lennie
fed the chickens,

chopped firewood

and milked the cows.

Then he harnessed the horses and ploughed the chocolate soil.

Each night Lennie fell into a deep, bone-weary sleep.

When Lennie's dad came home, he could see that Lennie had done the work of a man. "I'm proud of you, Lennie, so proud, I think you deserve a reward."
Lennie fidgeted for a moment. Could he ask?

Lennie took a deep breath. “I’d like to see the opening of the Sydney Harbour Bridge.”

“Well, perhaps we can find money for the train.”

“I’d like to ride Ginger Mick, Dad.”

Lennie’s dad scratched his chin, a sure sign he was making an important decision.

“All the way to Sydney? That’s a tall order – but if you managed the farm, I have no doubt you can do this.”

Lennie knew that if he travelled twenty miles a day he would make it on time and it wouldn't be too much for Ginger Mick.

So, on 3rd February 1932, when Lennie and Ginger Mick were nine years old, they set off along the winding road out of Leongatha, to ride six hundred miles to Sydney.

All went as planned till the third day out.

By midday the skies were dark and smoke hung thick and heavy. Bushfires were sweeping into nearby milling settlements and forests. Falling ash blocked their nostrils and stung their eyes.

The pony stopped and nickered.
"Come on, Ginger," Lennie whispered.

Lennie saw flames racing along the ridge.
He could hear the roaring rush of fire.

What should he do?

Lennie's heart was pounding and he knew Ginger's was too, but the trust they shared allowed Lennie to urge him on.

Somehow they made it to the small township of Kilmany, worn-out but safe.

They travelled on, winding north to the border of Victoria and New South Wales and into the rugged Snowy Mountains. Some days were hard and long, but always Lennie's dream was stronger than the challenge, as strong as Ginger's heart.

As the days passed they met other travellers, and swaggies searching for work.

“You’re the boy everyone’s talking about,” one said.

That wasn’t important to Lennie. He only wanted to see the bridge.

School children asked Lennie questions and fed Ginger Mick little treats.

In Canberra Lennie shook the hand of Prime Minister Joseph Lyons.

All along the way families offered them food and shelter and in some towns Lennie stayed for free in posh hotels.

But Lennie was happiest when they were by themselves and he could imagine what it would be like to reach the bridge.

Thirty-three days after leaving Leongatha, Lennie rode Ginger Mick down George Street in Sydney.

There it was. There was the incredible bridge reaching across the harbour.

Lennie knew it had been worth it, every mile and every one of Ginger's footsteps.

Lennie's grandfather met him on his way back home to the farm.

Left: Lennie; Above: Lennie and Ginger Mick

Tuesday 18th April 1922, Lennie Gwyther came into the world at Flers Farm near Leongatha. Close by a little foal was born.

The Sydney Harbour Bridge took almost nine years to build and employed 1654 workers at a time when Australia was in the grip of the Great Depression. The bridge gave its builders work, a purpose and involvement in the construction of Australia's most important and iconic structure.

Saturday 19th March 1932, a boy and his pony crossed Australia's Sydney Harbour Bridge and marched into history.

FOR THE BEST CHILDREN'S BOOKS, LOOK FOR THE BEAR.

BOB THE RAILWAY DOG
by Corinne Fenton
illustrated by Andrew McLean

The true story of a little dog who had adventure in his heart and the rattle of the rails in his soul.

In the early days of the railway, when shiny new tracks were opening vast areas of Australia, there was an adventurous dog who was part of it all. As the tracks were being laid he was there on the train - riding in his favourite spot on top of the Yankee engine. Everyone knew him. He was Bob the Railway Dog.

SHORTLISTED, FIVE TO EIGHT YEARS CATEGORY, SPEECH PATHOLOGY BOOK OF THE YEAR AWARDS, 2016

NOTABLE, PICTURE BOOK OF THE YEAR, CHILDREN'S BOOK COUNCIL OF AUSTRALIA (CBCA) AWARDS, 2016

"This delightful story of Bob will melt the hearts of the readers"
ReadPlus

Paperback ISBN 978-1-925381-23-8

LITTLE DOG AND THE SUMMER HOLIDAY
by Corinne Fenton
illustrated by Robin Cowcher

A charming and nostalgic story about a much-loved Little Dog and his family.

The summer holidays stretch out forever. Little Dog and his family set off with their caravan. A delightful story about the way family holidays used to be.

"This gorgeous, nostalgic story of an Australian holiday from the summer of 1957/58 is a must for all families."
Liz Derouet

Praise for *Little Dog and the Christmas Wish*

"If there is such a thing as a perfect 'grandparents' book', this is it."
The Australian

Paperback ISBN 978-1-760651-63-3

THE DOG ON THE TUCKERBOX
by Corinne Fenton
illustrated by Peter Gouldthorpe

The Dog on the Tuckerbox is the story of Australia's early pioneers, a time when the bullockies who worked the rough tracks needed a mate they could rely on. It is the story of Lady and her unwavering loyalty to her master, Bill.

NOTABLE BOOK, PICTURE BOOK OF THE YEAR, CBCA AWARDS, 2009

NOTABLE BOOK, EVE POWNALL AWARD FOR INFORMATION BOOKS, CBCA AWARDS, 2009

"This beautiful, thoughtful picture book depicts a lost time that is well worth revisiting . . ."
Magpies magazine

". . . will remain with the reader long after the book is closed."
The Canberra Times

Paperback ISBN 978-1-922077-46-2